A BOOK
FROM THE LIBRARY

Written by Clive Hopwood
Illustrated by Paul Crompton

Copyright © 1989 Thames Television Limited.
All rights reserved.
Published in Great Britain by World International Publishing Limited,
An Egmont Company, Egmont House, P.O. Box 111, Great Ducie Street, Manchester M60 3BL.
Printed in DDR. ISBN 7235 1357 0
2nd Reprint

The summer is over. The leaves are falling from the trees. The nights are growing dark sooner. Zippy looks out of the window and sighs.

"Why does it have to go dark so early?" asks Zippy. "I want to go out and play football."

"It's autumn," says Bungle.

"Well I don't like it," says Zippy. "Why can't it be summer all the year round?"

"That wouldn't be fair," says George.

"Why not?" asks Zippy.

George thinks. "If it was summer here all the time," he says, "it would have to be winter all the time somewhere else. That's not very fair."

Zippy still wants it to be summer.
He wants to play in the garden,
but it's too dark.

"Never mind," says Bungle. "We
can play indoors."

Zippy is still not happy. "I don't want to play indoors. I want to play football."

He sits down and sulks. "I'm bored," he says.

George and Bungle try to cheer him up. George brings over a game.

"Let's play *Snakes and Ladders*, Zippy," he says. That's fun to play."

Zippy does not want to join in. "I don't want to play *Snakes and Ladders*," says Zippy. "I want to play football. Take it away, George."

Bungle goes over to Zippy. He has a colouring book.

"You can colour in a picture, Zippy," says Bungle, "in my new colouring book."

Zippy is very hard to please. "I don't want to do any colouring," he says, "I want to play football."

He sits and stares out of the window.

Bungle and George are worried.
Zippy doesn't want to play
anything.
Then George has a good idea.

"Let's ask Geoffrey," says George.

Bungle nods. "He's sure to know what to do," says Bungle. "Come on, Zippy."

Bungle and George take Zippy to see Geoffrey.

Geoffrey is sitting in an armchair. He is reading a book. He doesn't see Bungle, George and Zippy come into the room.

Suddenly he laughs very loudly.

"Are you all right, Geoffrey?" asks George.

Geoffrey looks up. "Oh yes," he says. "It's this book I'm reading. It's very funny. It makes me laugh."

Geoffrey looks at Zippy. "What's the matter Zippy?" he asks.

"I'm bored," says Zippy.

"He wants to play football," says Bungle.

"But it's too dark," says George.

"And if it's dark," says Bungle.
"And if you can't think of
anything else to play," says
George.
"What do you do?" asks Zippy.

Geoffrey smiles. "What do I do," he says, "if I'm bored?"

"Or fed up?" asks Bungle.

"Or down in the dumps?" says George.

"I pick up a good book," says Geoffrey. "Then I curl up somewhere nice and warm and have a read."

Everyone looks at Zippy.

"I've read all my books," says Zippy. "I don't want to read them again."

"Read a new book then, Zippy," says George.

"I haven't got enough money,"
says Zippy, "to buy a new book."
"We can go to the library," says
Geoffrey. "You can borrow books
for free from there. Come on."

Geoffrey, George, Bungle and Zippy arrive at the library. It is still open.

The lady behind the desk is very helpful. She gives Zippy some tickets.

"For each ticket," she says, "you can borrow a book to take away and read. There are all kinds of books here. Story books, picture books. All kinds."

Zippy looks on the shelves. There
are lots of shelves and lots of
books. The lady helps him choose.
   She stamps the date on the books
and takes the tickets.

Zippy is very happy now.
"What books have you got?"
asks George.
Zippy smiles and shows him. All
the books are about football!